MADE TO LOVE YOU

LATOYA NICOLE

MADE TO LOVE YOU   LATOYA NICOLE

DEDICATIONS

THANK YOU TO ALL OF MY DEDICATED READERS. I APPRECIATE YOU FROM THE BOTTOM OF MY HEART FOR STICKING WITH ME THROUGH IT ALL. MOST OF MY BOOKS WERE TAKEN DOWN, BUT I HAVE SOME OF MY BOOKS COMING BACK TO YOU THIS MONTH. BE ON THE LOOK OUT. MAKE SURE YOU SUPPORT THOSE RERELEASES. DOWNLOAD THEM, READ THEM, AND TELL A FRIEND TO TELL A FRIEND. I DEFINITELY NEED ALL THE SUPPORT BACK ON MY INDIE RELEASES.

JONAY...

Grabbing the hot wings off the stove, I took them to the table in the living room. My best friend Nautica was in there getting our drinks ready. No matter what, we had a girl's night every Friday. Today, I needed the drink more than ever. My ass was stressed and since I didn't have a man, this was the only way I could release it.

"Bitch, them mufuckas look fye. So, what you gone do?" She asked as she dipped one in the ranch and started sucking on it like she hadn't eaten in years.

"I don't know. They told me they would contact me if another job became available, but I gotta find me somewhere permanent. This temp shit is for the birds." Grabbing some wings and putting them on my plate, I started eating with her. It was days like this I wish I had gotten my degree. My ass went to college for like a year in Administration, but my bills was kicking my ass, so I had to stop and get a job.

I assumed it was a lot of Administrative Assistant jobs, so I dropped out only to be out here struggling to find work. The temp agency kept me working for the most part, but the assignment could end without notice and that shit fucked me up every time. I really wanted to be hired on full time at my last one, because it had paid the most out of all my temp places. Fifteen dollars an hour wasn't a whole lot, but it was enough for me to be comfortable and pay my shit.

"You could always come and work with me. You know the dollars stay coming in at club Midnight." Rolling my eyes, I took a sip of some wine and went back to eating. I loved Nautica, but I swear she was always trying to get me to strip. Hell, I didn't even have the body for it and it just wasn't my cup of tea. Niggas wanted a chick with a lot of ass, and even though I had some nice curves on my slim frame, it was far from a stripper body.

"Naw bitch, you got that. I prefer to work a nine to five. Something gotta shake soon, or imma have to consider shaking this lil booty."

"Lil booty lives matter. It's some niggas in there that like that lil shit. Don't turn yo nose up at it, until you try it. Come by on amateur night and see how you like it." She must have had more drinks than I realized. There was no way I was getting on stage shaking my ass for everyone to see.

"I'm good, plus don't come for my ass like you didn't go to the DR and buy yours." Shrugging her shoulders, she grabbed another wing like it was nothing.

"Hey, it was an investment. That ass got me ugly paid and out the hood. My 2019 truck is paid for and I own my house. Like I said, don't knock it til you try it." My eyes damn near fell out of my head. I knew she was paid, but I ain't know she was getting it like that.

"Damn bitch, you didn't say stripping paid like that."

"It don't. It pays good, but most of my money comes from my side deals. All the ballers be in that bitch ready to pay for the pussy. Instead of fucking them for free, I charge them out the ass. One nigga wanna buy me a business, but I'm not trying to have ties to him like that. I'm just saying, it's power in the pussy if you use it." Laughing, I took another sip.

"You know damn well I ain't about to be fucking no nigga for money. Hell, it's been two years since I last had sex."

"Yeah I know. You're twenty four and if I didn't know you, I would swear you were fifty five. These are the years you supposed to be out here getting it in and fucking. Everybody know you can be a hoe up until you thirty. That's when you get your life together." I had no idea where she got her logic, but I swear the shit kept me laughing.

"Like I said, I'm good." We laughed and talked shit the rest of the night. It was good to take my mind off my problems for a while and my bitch always made sure she did that whenever we linked up.

****

Rushing, I pulled out all of my slacks that I had in my closet. I couldn't find my new pair of black pants, so I had to throw on a pair that was a little too tight. Buttoning up my white fitted shirt, I tucked it in and threw on my pink heels and grabbed my pink wristlet. Applying a light coat of makeup, I put on my pink YSL lipstick and I was ready. I hated running behind, but I had no idea they were going to contact me that fast about a new job. I was in no position to turn it down, so I jumped my ass up rushing to make it downtown.

The traffic was terrible, and I damn near had tears in my eyes as it got closer to the time I was supposed to have my meeting. I knew parking was going to kill me out, but that hot twenty was going to be worth it. This job at Hotel Ross was going to pay nineteen dollars an hour and it was for a couple of months. Finally pulling up, I jumped out the car and ran inside with literally one minute to spare.

The hotel was new, and I could tell the owner spent a bag because it was nice as hell. Everything was gold accented and I'm not sure if it was real crystal, but I loved the theme. I was broke as hell, but a bitch felt like royalty walking inside. I was shocked to see that it was empty, so I stood there looking dumb trying to find someone to help me. I didn't want to end up late, but that shit was looking inevitable. A white guy finally walked out of the back and I was shocked at his attire. For this to be an upscale hotel, his ass had on a hoodie and some jeans. Even though he was dressed down, I noticed his shoes were custom Christian Louboutins.

"I'm sorry, but the hotel is not open to the public yet." His ass never looked at me and that pissed me off. That's how most white people were when they had money. They would dismiss the shit out of a broke mufucka in a minute. Throwing on my professional voice, I responded.

"I'm sorry, I think I'm supposed to meet someone in HR. I'm here for the assistant job. I was told to come." Finally, he looked up and it was weird. He just stood there staring at me and it made me feel uncomfortable. I've never been into the swirl, but he was fine as hell. He had this look about him that gave me bad boy vibes. Even though his hair was low, it was enough to be in a wild look. A bushy fade I think you would call it. It was a brownish red color and he had a full beard covering his face and that alone was sexy. The diamonds in his ear was subtle, but you could tell they were expensive. The tats all over his arms had me ready to say fuck it and give his ass some of this black pussy, but I laughed the thought away.

"I'm Leiland, what's your name?" He walked over to me never taking his eyes off me. When I dropped my head slightly, I could feel him roaming my body.

"I'm Jonay. Can you tell me where I would go to meet HR? I'm already late and Lord knows I need this job. I'm sure whoever is in charge of this mufucka want a bitch to be on time." I laughed, but he just continued to look at me.

Assuming he was working here like me, I thought I could open up and be myself. When he just stared at me, I realized that might not be the case.

"You don't need to go meet anyone. I can show you what you need to be doing. I need to head out for a few, so you can do the shit I was handling. You need to make a few calls for me and go grab some shit for me as well. I'll give you a list of what I need and I'll check back in with you later to make sure you're good." Hearing this mufucka talk like me, let me know he was not the person I should have been meeting. Actually, I could look at him and tell that shit. He must have thought I was a goofy or something though. If he thought for one second he was going to push his work load on me, he had me fucked up.

"Naw see. That's not how this shit gone go. I'm here to do MY job, not yours. I'm not the help, mmk. Now, if you don't know who I should be meeting, just say that shit, but you not about to unload your shit on me. That's that white privilege bullshit." Rolling my eyes, I started walking towards

the desk to see if it was a bell or something.

"White privilege? Why, because I gave you an

assignment? How the fuck does that equal to me treating you

like the help? You just said you were here for a job, correct?" I

was trying to be nice, but I guess he was going to try me

today.

"I came here for my job. Not to do yours. If you don't

mind, I'll rather wait for the person in charge." Dismissing

him, I turned back towards the counter.

"Shorty, I don't know who you-..." I cut him off right

there.

"My name is Jonay. Not shorty."

"And my name is Leiland-..." Cutting him off again, I

gave him all the attitude I could muster up.

"You already told me your name. If you haven't figured

it out by now, this conversation is over." He was fine and all, but I didn't take disrespect or mufuckas trying to use me lightly.

"Rosstein." I was lost.

"What?"

"I'm Leiland Rosstein. Hence Hotel Ross. It don't get no bigger than me baby, I'm the owner." My eyes popped out my head and my heart shot through my ass. Knowing an apology would never make up for how I talked to him, I just turned around and ran out the door. I didn't stop running until I made it to my car and that shit was hard as hell to do in them heels. I couldn't believe I talked to the owner of the hotel like that. Granted, he looked nothing like you would expect an owner to look like, but I guess that's why you never judge a book by its cover. Knowing I blew the hell out of that job, I put my car in drive and took off. Heading back home, I let the tears flow. I didn't know how I was going to pay my bills this month, but I prayed the temp agency called me with another job.

LEILAND...

The look on Jonay's face when she found out I was the owner was priceless. It was always the look I got from anyone when they found out I was the mufucka in charge. Nothing about me looked like an upper class boujie white boy and that was because I wasn't. I grew up on the westside of Chicago and my parents struggled like anyone else's. Just like a typical teenager from the hood, I got in the streets and started selling drugs. Before long, I was selling drugs to rich white boys willing to pay top dollar for my product.

Of course, the color of my skin granted me help from people in higher places. One of my customers taught me how to invest my bread, and that shit paid off. Big. The more I made, the more I put in stocks. By the time I was twenty one, I no longer needed to sell drugs. Hell, I could do nothing for the rest of my life if I managed it right, but it wasn't until I got stock in Amazon and this internet company that took me to new heights. At Twenty five years old, I was worth two hundred million and suddenly I was somebody. Everyone forgot that I was poor white trash and everybody who was anybody wanted in my circle. Wanting to have something I could leave to my kids one day, I decided to build a hotel. My girl Stacie was helping me with the grand opening we were doing on Valentine's Day and she broke her leg. Grabbing my phone, I called her.

"Hey hunny, how is everything going?" She always sounded so chipper and I'm guessing it was because Stacie never seen a hard day in her life. I don't know why, but that shit annoyed the hell out of me.

"It's good. Why didn't you call me and tell me you sent a replacement? I was in here looking dumb as hell when she walked in." I could hear her giggle and I waited for her to respond.

"Because I wanted to surprise you. I know you have a lot on your plate, so I sent someone to help. I'm sure she is not as competent as me, but you can send me over her work and I'll give the okay first."

"That makes no sense to me. Why would I pay her to do a job, then send the shit to you? That's costing me more time, make the shit make sense."

"What did I tell you about speaking that way. You're not in the ghetto anymore, so stop trying to act like you are. If you feel she is good enough to finish the job, then that's perfect. I'll probably be back before it's all done anyway. What's she like? Is she cute?" I could hear the jealousy in her voice, but I was not about to pacify her.

"She's definitely sexy." The line went quiet and I could tell she was trying to figure out if I was joking or not. "I need the address she has on file for my records. Can you get that for me and call me back?"

"What's her name?" Her attitude was jumping through the phone.

"All I know is Jonay. I have no records or no way to add her into payroll. So, I'm going to need you to send all of that over. When she laughed, I was confused.

"Oh, she's black. Why didn't you say that? Had me over here worried. I'll send you over the information shortly." Before I could curse her ass out, she hung up. Stacie was implying she had nothing to worry about because Jonay was black, but she had every reason to worry.

As soon as I looked up at her, my dick bricked up. Shorty was probably the sexiest female I had ever laid eyes on. She was tall with a small frame, but I could tell it wasn't from working out. It was curvy, but she definitely wasn't thick. Jonay was a chocolate complexion and that shit looked smooth as hell and her full lips had me wanting to feel them around my dick. I've never dated a black girl before and it's not that I didn't want to. When I was growing up, they always looked at me as the dirty white boy trying to be black. When I started getting money, white women tended to flock to me. At that point, I just wanted some pussy, so that was who I dated.

Five minutes later, I heard the fax machine going off and I grabbed the papers out of it. I needed her address and that was the only way I knew how to get it from Stacie. As soon as Jonay found out who I was, she took off without letting me say a word. Nothing she said bothered me, I was used to the shit. People love to prejudge me and that was cool. I didn't lose any sleep or any bread behind that shit, so it didn't bother me at all. I did want her to know that I wasn't like that though. She could be herself around me, hell I preferred it. All day I was surrounded by people trying to kiss my ass because of who I was. It would be refreshing to have a real mufucka around. Jumping in my Porsche, I headed towards her house.

Pulling up to the building she lived in, I jumped out and walked up to the second floor. When I knocked on the door, I could hear cursing and laughing. To someone else in my circle, it would have sounded ghetto and ratchet, but the shit was music to my ears. My house was always so quiet, but I wasn't raised like that. Me and my brothers stayed in one room and we were always joking and talking shit with each other. Now, everyone was on a high horse like we didn't come from the hood. Knocking on the door, I waited for someone to answer. When they did, it wasn't Jonay, but some other girl. I'm not gone lie, she was fine as hell with a banging ass body, but I knew a fake ass when I saw one.

"Bitch either you going to jail, or you're being audited. Which one?" I wanted to laugh and tell her neither, but before I could, Jonay came to the door and I just knew she could see my dick about to push her over it was so hard. She had changed into some leggings and a tank. She wasn't wearing a bra, so her nipples were poking out of her shirt. It took everything in me not to put one in my mouth.

"Mr. Rosstein, what are you doing here?"

"This is the boss you cursed out? You didn't tell me he was white. He here to get your ass locked up." This time I did laugh.

"Naw I'm not on that. I came to ask why you leave? Last time I checked, you're not off the clock until seven. Imma need you to come back to the hotel. You don't have to change though you can dress how you want to." She looked shocked and her friend did too.

"You're going to let me keep my job after how I talked to you?" Shrugging, I leaned against the door frame.

"Why not? You said what you felt. Shid, if I thought someone was trying to get over on me, I would have cursed them the fuck out as well. Look, as much as I would like to stand here and shoot the shit with you, I have a lot of shit to do today. I really need you at the hotel helping me out. I know parking high, so you can roll with me and I'll drop you off later." She looked over at the other girl as if she was asking permission.

"Bitch fuck you looking at me for? I can't pay your bills, unless you about to go with me and shake some ass, you gone need to go your ass with him and work. I'll call you later and see how your first day went and if massa worked you to death." Laughing again, I shook my head as she walked past me. She made sure she was close enough to feel me breathing. Her ass brushed up against me and I shook my head. I hated to see fine women be out there thirsty. Shit wasn't cute.

"Let me throw on some shoes and a shirt."

"Just throw on some shoes, I gotta get out of here." I said that faster than I wanted to, but the creep in me wanted to look at her nipples all day.

"It's cold as hell outside, you trying to give me pneumonia. It will only take a second." When she walked off, I cursed Chicago weather. I hope her shirt was fitted and she left the bra off. As soon as she headed back out I knew her bra was on. Shit was sitting up too nice. I waited for her to lock the door and we went downstairs and got in my car. "Damn, must be nice." Looking over at her, I laughed. She really did say the first thing that came to her mind.

"It is." Taking off fast, I jumped on 290 and headed back down town. She leaned forward and turned on my radio. I could tell she was surprised to see Rick Ross playing. "Oh, you one of those." Now, I was irritated.

"One of what?" She looked at me nervous as if she was scared to speak her mind in fear of getting fired. "Let's get this straight, I don't need another yes man. You can say what's on yo mind and I won't fire you. As long as you're doing your job and you don't disrespect me, we good."

"I'm saying you one of those white boys that thinks he's black or like to act black. Like it's the in thing to do." Scrolling my phone, I went to my playlist and hit play. 7 Years by Lukas Graham started playing.

"So, am I trying to be white now?" When she didn't respond, I shook my head and started laughing. "I don't try to be anything. I love music, all kinds, but if you must know I grew up on the rap shit." Her face expression led me to believe she thought I was lying.

"If you say so." Not bothering to dignify that with a response, I turned my shit back to Rick Ross and blasted that shit.

JONAY...

Today seemed extra long after the ride back to the hotel with Leiland. His ass was feeling some kind of way, but I have no idea why. He said I could be honest and I'm sure he was used to people saying that. From the way he talked and dressed, it seemed as if he was trying to be something he wasn't. Yeah, I've seen white boys with swag, hell I even wanted a few, but nothing like this before. If his ass was rich enough to buy a damn hotel, he damn sure wasn't one of those white boys from the hood.

I hated pretenders. My black ass was out here struggling and mufuckas like him wanted to act like us. Take this credit score and these bills. It was funny how white people tried to be us, but blacks weren't afforded the opportunity to pretend like we were them. I'll take an eight hundred credit score any day and gladly eat casserole.

Laughing at my own joke, I finished placing my order for the table and chair covers.

At first, I thought this was going to be hard, but I realized I was actually good at event planning. Not only was I getting everything together for the party, but I was handling all the stuff he didn't get a chance to get for the rooms. The place was really nice and I wish I could afford to stay here. Just as I had the thought, he walked in. His ass been gone all day and I didn't even get a chance to take a lunch. My car was at home and I was broke anyway.

"Hey, do we get employee discounts on the rooms? I would like to stay here in the future sometimes, but I can't afford this shit."

"Don't worry about it. You can stay whenever you want to free of charge." I wanted to be happy, but I felt a way that he didn't even look up at me. Trying to break the tension, I decided to talk about work. "Can you come with me upstairs, so I can show you what I want to do."

"Yeah, give me a minute. Let me finish this email up first." I don't know why, but his demeanor towards me was bothering me. I know I said he was trying to be something he wasn't, but at least that mufucka had personality and kept me entertained. As of now, he really was treating me like the help and I didn't like it. I wanted to see his smile and hear his laugh, instead, all I got was his ass to kiss. That email took him twenty minutes and then he walked towards the elevator without saying a word. Biting my tongue, I walked over to where he was. When we got on, he didn't even look at me. "What floor we going to?"

"Anyone it don't matter." When he pushed one, he went back to looking at his phone. Walking off, he used some master key and opened the door. All the rooms had one bedroom or more, so the room we were standing in was basically the living room. It didn't have that cheap small couch like most hotels, it was big and plush. The kind you could fall asleep on and not want to get up. "So, I was thinking-…" When I saw he was still in his phone, I walked in his face and grabbed it from him.

"Fuck you do that for?"

"If you don't want to be bothered, fine. We can go back downstairs, but if you say you want to know my ideas, then at least you can do is respect me enough to listen."

"I am listening, all you said was you were thinking. I didn't know I had to look at you to hear you." His ass was being funny and he knew it.

"Okay, let's get this out of the way. What I said was out of line and I'm sorry. I would very much appreciate if we could go back to the way we were before I said all of that."

"You said what you meant, it's good. Now, what were you thinking?"

"They have these see through mini refrigerators and I think it will go more with the theme of the room. Everything else in here is boujie, why have the same old ass mini fridges? Oh, and I think instead of the mini bar, do like a wine cooler type of thing. Also, no matter how nice the room is, it's never

anything on tv. So, I want to replace all the TVs in the rooms

with smart TVs giving them the option to log into Netflix and

stuff."

"Bet. Order all the shit and use the company checks."

My eyes damn near popped out of my head.

"You don't want to use a credit card or something?

That shit could be expensive."

"It's good. Just make sure you put the receipts with the

other ones when you're done. Did you get all the stuff ordered

for the party?" My feelings was hurt, I expected him to be a

little more excited.

"Yeah, I did. If you don't mind, can you take me home

now. You left, so I didn't get a chance to eat anything and I'm

starving."

"Yup." Just like that, he walked out the door. If I didn't

need this money, I would leave and not come back. He was

being a jerk on purpose and I didn't know how to take that.

When we got back downstairs, I grabbed my coat and we walked out in silence. As soon as my ass hit the seat, he turned the radio all the way up and drove off fast as hell. When we pulled up at my house, he got out and opened my door.

"Work starts at nine. I'll text you my number just in case you need me." Before I could respond, he got in the car and drove off. Nautica came walking up as I made it to my front door and I needed an ear right now.

"How did your first day go on the plantation with massa? Did you eat tuna casserole for lunch?" Laughing, I washed my hands and went to the fridge to find something quick to eat.

"Hell naw, I didn't eat shit. He got mad at me on the way there and the nigga left me all day by myself."

"Bitch what did you say to him now? I know you think you can say whatever comes the fuck up, but he's still your boss dummy." Opening one of my salads, I sat down and poured the dressing on.

"I know. I kind of told him he was trying to be black because he was listening to Rick Ross." Nautica started choking on her juice and I fell out laughing. "What, he said I can be myself and say what I wanted, so that's what I did. The minute the shit left my lips, his entire demeanor changed."

"You owe him an apology. Girl, you don't know what that man been through and you out here acting like the judge and the jury. Even if he is pretending, who the fuck are you to tell him he is? Do better before yo slow ass be fired." She was right, but I didn't want to hear it. Don't tell me I can say what I want, but get mad when I do.

"I'm there to do a job, not be his friend. I'll get through the day without him talking to me."

"You got issues. Do you think he like black girls, I wouldn't mind riding his face? That nigga is fine."

"Eww you nasty as hell. I don't know, and he's not talking to me, so I can't ask him."

"Bitch a dick is a dick and a rich one is even better. Fuck you talking about. You better wake up and smell the vanilla bean." Shaking my head, I laughed at her for the rest of the night.

LEILAND...

I know I was acting like a dick towards Jonay, but that shit pissed me off. Here I was trying to explain to her who I was, but she was just fine throwing my ass in a box. Shorty thought she had me all figured out and I wanted to show her who I was. I guess it was going the way that it should have been since I had a girl. The thoughts I was having about Jonay wasn't ones I should be having. Me and my girl had been together four years and this was the first time another chick had even caught my eye.

We didn't have the best relationship, but I wasn't the type to cheat. If I was in, I was all in that bitch, but Jonay had me feeling differently. Every time I looked at her, my dick bricked up. I was a grown ass man and I knew how to control my hormones, but not around Jonay. Here I was trying to figure out ways to get to know her, but she was treating me like she had me all figured out. It didn't even dawn on me that I drove her there, so she couldn't eat lunch. Most people called Uber Eats or some shit, but I wasn't trying to starve her ass. Pulling up to my downtown loft, I drove in the parking garage and got out. Walking inside, I shook my head at Stacie in the kitchen trying to cook. Not only did she cook like a typical white girl, but she was struggling on her one leg. She knew I hated her food, but she was trying anyway and that was part of the reason I stayed with her.

"Hey baby, I was trying to be done before you got here. How was your first day without me?" Walking over, I pecked her on the cheek and looked to see what she was making. Looked like stove top and boiled chicken. I've told her over and over that shit ain't dressing, but she insisted that it was. Looking at her, I realized she was damn near naked and my dick didn't make a move. I saw Jonay's nipple through a shirt and almost exploded on myself.

"It was straight. Shorty fixed the rooms up better she had some great ideas." I could tell she didn't like that, but it was the truth.

"What do you mean better?"

"Just more up to date with stuff. Look, I'm tired I'm about to go take a shower and go to sleep. I've had a long day." I could tell she wanted me to sit, eat, and talk with her, but I was tired as fuck. Plus, I wasn't eating that bland ass shit. When we first got together, I did because I thought it was polite, but for the past three years I've told her I was straight. We eat out damn near every day, but every now and then she wants to try and cook again. I even hired cooks, but she always fire them saying they cook ghetto.

Taking my clothes off, I climbed in the overhead shower and let that shit run all over my body. Today went perfect, but I was still stressed the fuck out and I knew why. Jonay was running her ass through my thoughts and I couldn't shake the shit. Just me saying her name in my mind had my dick bricking up. Doing something I hadn't done in years, I started stroking my shit. I had a good rhythm going when I heard Stacie.

"Oh my god, are you jacking off?"

"Naw, I'm cleaning my dick. Can you get the fuck out? Damn!?

"Why are you talking to me like this? All I wanted to do was hear about your day. I'm sure most of the stuff didn't get done since you didn't have competent help, so I'm just trying to see what I could do." That shit pissed me off to no end.

"So, you automatically think she's incompetent because she's black? Imma ask you again to get the fuck out and let me wash my ass. I can't deal with yo ignorance tonight."

"It's your and excuse me if I don't want you talking like you're from the ghetto. Or that I don't want to trust our million dollar hotel with a girl from the ghetto." Oh yeah, she had lost her fucking mind.

"It's what the fuck I say it is and did you forget YO slow ass the one that hired her and it's MY million dollar hotel. If you don't get the fuck out, I will." Rolling her eyes, she hopped out of the bathroom. Washing up, I got out and went in the guest room. Grabbing my phone, I decided to text Jonay.

ME: this is my number store me in.

NAY: Got it and thank you again for the opportunity.

ME: You can stop kissing ass, I told you I won't fire you. If you want to kiss something I can think of other places, I ain't with that gay shit.

NAY: Fuck you!

Laughing, I turned my phone off and just stared at the ceiling. When Stacie sent over all her info, I stored her number right away. I knew that shit was going to get me in trouble, but I said what the fuck. Grabbing my phone again, I

texted back.

ME: Don't write a check yo ass can't cash.

It was hell staring at the phone waiting on the bubble

to pop up. Right when I was about to give up, it popped up

and I couldn't do shit but smile.

NAY: Go to sleep. We have a long day ahead of us

tomorrow. This time, try not to starve me.

ME: I got you.

This time when I laid the phone down, I didn't pick it

back up. I wasn't going to push my luck tonight. She was gone

have to see me tomorrow though.

****

Getting out of my Rolls truck, I walked up the two

flights to Jonay's apartment. I was hoping she hadn't already

left because I was sure she was gone try to ride the train.

Parking was a bitch downtown and I was sure she didn't think

to park in the hotel lot. I wasn't going to tell her if I was able to pick her up every day. Knocking on the door, I hoped she answered.

"Mr. Rosstein, what are you doing here? Am I late?" She was dressed down today in some jeans and a sweater, and I could tell she went without a bra today.

"My name is Leiland, and I'm here to take you to work. I know how expensive parking can be. You ready?"

"Let me grab my purse and my coat." I waited for her to grab her things and she locked her door and we headed downstairs. When she saw my truck, I could tell she was biting back what she wanted to say. Opening her door, I let her in and then walked to my side and got in.

"Just get it over with and say it?" Shaking her head no, she started looking in her purse for something. "You can say it."

"The last time I said what I was thinking, you didn't talk to me the rest of the day and starved me, I'm good."

Laughing, I decided to be petty with her and threw on some Sam Smith.

"Okay for real, how many cars do you have?"

"Ten cars, five trucks, and two bikes." Her eyes damn near popped out of her head.

"This might be rude as fuck, but how much are you worth? I mean, I could just google it, but it be wrong sometimes."

"After the hotel, about two hundred." I could see her relax.

"Oh, that's not bad. You might want to slow down on buying all these expensive cars and stuff though. I'm not gone lie I could do a lot with two hundred thousand dollars." Now it was my turn to laugh.

"Million." Her mouth made an O shape, but nothing came out. The rest of the way was quiet and I managed to steal a few glances. Shorty was that natural pretty and I loved that about her. If I hugged Stacie, I was gone walk away with her face on my shirt. I pulled in front of the hotel and parked. If I went in the lot, she would think to drive.

"Let me get to work. What are we going to do about lunch?" She was always talking about eating it seemed like.

"I'll take you somewhere, but take your coat off and come upstairs with me real quick. I wanna get your thoughts on something." She did what I asked and followed me over to the elevator. When we got on the floor, I opened one of the rooms and walked inside.

"We were just in here yesterday, if you wasn't being an ass, you could have asked me then." I wanted to tell her I couldn't see her nipples yesterday, so sex wasn't on my mind, but I didn't.

"Just shut the fuck up for once. Sit on the bed for me and tell me what you feel." She looked confused, but she did it.

"It feels like a damn good mattress."

"Yeah, but do you think it's one of those good sex mattresses? I've been to some hotels that had the kind of bed that made it hard as hell to beat a pussy up in. I don't want that for my shit, so what you think?" She laughed, but started bouncing on it trying to see.

"I don't know. I'm guessing I would have to be having sex or I need another body to figure it out."

"May I?" This time her eyes did fall out of her head. I wanted to laugh, but I was dead serious. My beds had to be perfect for everything.

"May you get in bed with me?" The way she said it had my dick bricking up again.

"Not like on no freaky shit. I really just want to make sure couples can fuck in my beds."

"Okay." It was barely above a whisper, but I heard her. I'm sure she meant lying beside her, but I laid on top of her and started bouncing. Her nipples were rubbing against me and I knew it wouldn't be long before I embarrassed myself.

"Seems like it has good traction to me. You have nothing to worry about Leiland, everything is going to be perfect." I knew that was my cue to get up, but I was stuck staring at her. As soon as I thought I needed to move, it happened. My dick was harder than a pimp slap. I was hoping she didn't feel it, but I could see it in her face that she did.

"Uhhmmm ummm." Jonay cleared her throat and I came out of my trance.

"My bad." Climbing off her, I tried to look everywhere but in her direction.

"What do you need me to do today?" Suck my dick.

"It's a list downstairs on the desk. I need you to make sure all of them agree to coming to the grand opening."

"Okay." When she walked out, I stayed behind and jacked off on them high ass blankets. This girl was driving me crazy.

JONAY...

"We could have eaten lunch at the hotel, you didn't have to bring me out. I ain't gone lie though, this food banging." I had this mac and cheese with sausage in it that had me ready to slap somebody mama.

"You said you've never even seen the inside of The Rain Forest Café, I had to bring you here. I've eaten everywhere down this bitch, trust me, this is nothing." Shaking my head, I smiled at him.

"I'm sure. Hell, I'm surprised yo rich ass will even eat in a spot like this."

"I'll eat anywhere if the food is good. Now hurry yo fat ass up, so I can drop you off at home." Taking my last bite slowly, I licked my fork and laughed at his face expression. If I didn't know any better, I would have thought I turned Leiland on. He constantly stared at me and when we were trying out his mattress, I'm sure I felt his dick get hard. Not one to play themselves, I kept that thought in my head. There was no way a mufucka like him wanted a little nobody like me.

"You better stop doing that shit if you want me to keep being a gentleman." Deciding to play with his ass just to see how far he would go, I kept licking.

"What you gone do Leiland?" His smile left his face and he stared at me intense as hell.

"Jonay, I'm asking you not to play with me. Unless you ready to get this dick dropped off in you, keep yo tongue in yo mouth." Before I could respond, someone interrupted us.

"Fancy seeing you here." Leiland just stared at her. "Son, that is not the way to treat your mother. Show some manners, stand up and greet me." He wiped his mouth and stood up.

"What's up ma." When he kissed her cheek, she grimaced.

"Quit speaking like you're unaware of how to speak proper English. Who is your little friend and where is Stacie?"

I had no idea who Stacie was, but that comment pissed him off.

"I can talk how the fuck I want to and last I checked, you from the same hood as me. My money give you status, don't forget that. This is Jonay and we're on lunch. If you don't mind, I would like to get back to eating my food." Giving an oh expression, his mother reached out her hand and I shook it.

"I'm Nancy, I'm sorry I didn't realize you were someone that works with my son. Please forgive his ways. For some reason, he wishes to remind himself and others of a horrible time in our lives. I'll let you get back to your meal, I'm just here meeting a friend."

"It's nice to meet you ma'am." When Leiland didn't say anything, I kept eating my food unsure of what to do next.

"Do you mind getting that to go?" Shaking my head no, I waited for them to bring us a couple of boxes. As soon as we were back in the car, I looked over to him but he was in deep thought.

"What did you mean she grew up in the same hood as you?" He finally looked at me and I could tell he was trying to see if he wanted to open up to me.

"We grew up probably about five minutes from you on sixteenth. The same ghetto as the next. The same struggle and everything else. That's why it pisses me off when someone try to insinuate I'm pretending to be black. My upbringing was just as black as yours." I was shocked and I never would have guessed it. No wonder his swag and the way he talk was black as hell. If you weren't looking at him, you would have sworn his ass was black.

"Again, I'm sorry for that."

"It's good. You didn't know, but now you do. Now that I have bread, everyone seems to forget where the fuck we come from and they the ones pretending they something they ain't. Shit be blowing me."

"Don't ever let anyone tell you who you should be. If you're comfortable like this, no amount of money should be able to change that. At the end of the day, you're Leiland. Fuck them. I've learned to stop dumbing myself down for other people." He didn't say anything, but I can tell he understood what I meant. We pulled up to my house and he got out as usual and opened my door. When he closed it and started walking me to the door, I looked at him like he was crazy. "Mufucka do you know they will steal yo shit?" Laughing, he opened the door for me and walked me inside.

"If they do, I guess a mufucka spending the night. Plus, I got more it's good." I would die if someone stole my damn Nissan Altima.

"I bet you would want to spend the night wouldn't you?" I was running up the stairs, but I turned to make sure he was still behind me he got so quiet. When I got to the door, he walked up close to me. Too close.

"You have no idea how much I wanna spend the night with you." I couldn't do shit but breathe and look at him like he lost his mind. His hand started slowly going up my shirt and I was frozen in time. Leiland's fingers started caressing my nipples and my eyes closed ,and for the moment, I sat there and enjoyed it. My pussy was waking up, but I knew I couldn't do this.

"I can't. I'm sorry." Turning around, I unlocked my door and ran inside. I couldn't control my breathing and I swear I was lost on how the hell this happened. When I heard the knocks on the door, I ignored them. Fuck that, because if I opened that bitch, I was going to give in. It's been so long since I had some, I wasn't equipped to turn down dick like that. Hearing my door open, I turned around quick as hell.

"Bitch I know you heard me knocking. Fuck wrong with you and why the hell yo titty hanging out of your shirt?" Looking down, I laughed as I fixed myself.

"You will not believe what the fuck just happened." Walking to the kitchen, I grabbed a bottle of wine and two cups. Taking them back in the front room to Nautica, I sat down and poured myself a glass.

"Are you going to tell me or are you gone sit here sipping and shit being dramatic?" Holding my finger up, I gulped down my wine and poured another glass.

"Dig this right, me and Leiland was talking on the way here and shit got kind of deep."

"Who in the fuck is Leiland?"

"Mr. Rosstein is Leiland. Anyway, he walk me upstairs right and I said something about them stealing his car and he was gone have to spend the night. This mufucka tell me he wants to stay with me and then start massaging my titties. I took off and ran in the house and then you was here." Drinking some more of my wine, I waited to see what she was going to say.

"Bitch, I told you find out if he liked black pussy. I ain't tell yo ass to give him yours. I wanted to know for me. Selfish ass. I want some of them rich balls too with yo stingy ass." Shaking my head, I couldn't believe she was making jokes right now.

"Can you be serious for once. Fuck am I going to do? He is my boss and now shit is going to be weird as hell. I don't want him like that and now his ass gone fire me when I tell him I'm good." She looked at me like I was crazy.

"Why the fuck you don't want him?"

"Umm bitch cus he white. The fuck." I looked at her as if she was losing her mind.

"Bitch all the money he got, that nigga is green. Since when you a racist?" Now I was offended.

"I'm not racist, I just ain't never been down with the swirl. How the fuck imma suck a pink dick? Yo ass tripping hard."

"Okay my country tis of thee looking ass. Everybody know you're black. It's nothing wrong with trying something new. Every Martin Luther King you dated dogged and beat yo ass. Better give ol Billy Bob Thornton a chance. That dick might change yo life. Again, if you don't want him though, tell him to call me. I'll throw this pussy all on that man."

"I'm sure you will bitch. It ain't too many niggas you won't throw that pussy on."

"Touché bitch." Taking another sip, I tried to figure out what the fuck I was going to do tomorrow.

LEILAND...

"What is wrong with you? It's like you done changed in the last few days. I'm trying to figure out what is going on with you, but you refuse to let me in. What's bothering you?" Grabbing my keys, I tried to get out of the house. Stacie was annoying the fuck out of my ass and I didn't want to hear it.

"How many times do I have to tell you ain't shit wrong with me. I got a lot of shit to do to make sure my shit right. If you wanted to help me maybe you shouldn't have broken yo fucking leg." She looked shocked and I didn't give a fuck.

"I broke my leg trying to carry in some boxes into your hotel. Don't act as if I did this on purpose. You're mad that I'm not there and I get that, just tell me what I can do to make it better." When she started moaning under her breath, I shook my head.

"Stacie, I'm good. I don't know why it's so hard for you to understand that, but I am. I just need to get to work and get started on my day. We'll fuck later, I'm not in the mood right now." To be honest, I haven't been in the mood since I met Jonay.

"Your mother called me yesterday. She told me you were slumming it with your employee and I'm starting to wonder if she's the reason you're in a bad mood. If she can't do the job, I will call the temp agency and have them send you someone else."

"NO! I mean it's good." I said that a lil stronger than I meant to. The last thing I wanted was for Jonay to disappear out of my life. She was actually the reason for my bad mood. Not because I was mad at her or anything, but she had my head all fucked up and I couldn't read her. She flirted with me all day and then the minute I made my move, she took off running again. I was just ready to be inside of her pussy at this point, but I knew I couldn't do that to her. I was in a relationship, so I needed to learn how to get my emotions in check.

"I'll see you later." Nodding, I walked out the door and didn't respond. I knew she was sad, but right now I had to leave if I wanted to make it to Jonay's house to pick her up. We would have workers in the hotel today, so I wanted to talk to her before we got there. I needed her to understand that nothing that happened would affect her job.

When I pulled up to her house, I sat in my Tesla for a minute trying to gather my thoughts. I had no idea what I wanted to say to her, but I knew I didn't want to say the wrong thing. Finally shaking the bitch off me, I jumped out and ran inside her building. Taking two steps at a time, I tried to get upstairs fast as hell. Knocking on her door, I waited for someone to answer but she didn't.

Either she wasn't going to work for me anymore or her ass was already gone. After what happened, I'm starting to think she took the train. Driving to the end of the line where she would get off, I sat there and waited. When she walked

onto the sidewalk, I swear I could see her walking in the

house to me after a long day of work. I don't know if she was

trying to impress me or if she was trying to keep it

professional, but she was looking good as fuck. She had on

some boots that went up to her thighs with some tight ass

jeans on. Some flowy ass jacket and a big ass scarf. If that

would have been Stacie, she would have been out here in

heels, pantyhose, and a damn dress like it ain't cold out this

bitch. Tapping the horn, she looked over but since she didn't

recognize my car, she kept walking.

"Jonay, can I talk to you for a minute?" It looked like

she rolled her eyes at me, but she came over. When she

climbed in the car I could tell she was pissed.

"So, you're stalking me now? If I wasn't at home for

you to pick me up, why would you drive around until you

found me? You're too smart not to catch the fucking hint."

Instead of getting pissed I laughed.

"It's too cold for you to be out here taking the train and I knew we needed to talk about last night. It will be all kind of people at the hotel, so I wanted to holla at you." Instead of being relieved, she exhaled all hard and shit.

"Now they are going to think I'm screwing my boss. If we walk in together or they see us sitting in the car talking, what will they think?" I really wanted to tell her I didn't give a fuck what they thought, I was paying them, but I didn't.

"Okay, you go inside and take a key. Text me what floor and room you went to and I will meet you there. Act like you need to do inventory or some shit. I'll see you in ten." She smiled, so I knew she liked that idea. As soon as I pulled up in the front, Jonay jumped out of my car. Driving around back, I took my time trying to procrastinate until I got her text. As soon as it came through, I walked inside. No one was paying attention to me or anybody else.

Everybody was working, but I didn't mind the privacy. Jumping on the elevator, I went upstairs to the room she texted and used my main key to get inside. Making sure the extra lock was on, I went over to the bed and sat next to her. She had removed her coat and scarf downstairs I assumed and I loved the fitted shirt she was wearing.

"You're very attractive, but you're not my type. Besides, you're my boss and we need to keep some boundaries between us. I'll get myself to and from work. It would be nice if you paid for lunch, but if you didn't, that would be fine." I heard her, but I wasn't trying to hear it. Leaning in close, I stared at her lips as I talked.

"So, you saying you don't want me." When she didn't respond, I took her lip in my mouth and sucked it. As soon as I released it, she started her shit.

"I can't do this. We were supposed to be up here talking. Not doing this again." Ignoring her, I reached in her shirt and pulled out one of her titties. Before she could protest, I had her nipple in my mouth sucking that bitch like I was attached. "Mmm fuck. This is wrong on so many levels."

"Shut the fuck up. I'm tired of hearing you whine. Just relax." Not giving her time to protest, I covered her mouth with mine and stuck my tongue inside. Jonay pushed me back, but when I looked at her, all I saw was desire and need for a mufucka. Taking my tongue, I ran it down her lips straight to the titty I had already pulled out. Not wanting to ask for permission or wait for her to start saying no again, I used my hand to undo her jeans. That shit wasn't easy since I was excited as fuck. Finally saying to hell with being nice about the shit, I leaned back and snatched her pants down with her panties in tow. Grabbing her leg, I unzipped one of her boots and then did the other. I never took my eyes off of her as I slid her shit all the way off. "Can I taste you?"

Her nasty ass wasn't fighting then. She shook her head fast as hell and I laughed to myself as I slid in between her legs. As soon as my tongue eased up her shit, her body started shaking. That shit only turned me on more, so I went in full attack mode. I went from sucking on her clit to fucking her pussy with my tongue. Shorty was grinding on my face hard as fuck and then out of nowhere she started convulsing. Knowing I couldn't let her take too long to recoup, I pulled my pants down fast as hell and guided my dick towards her pussy. I knew I needed a condom, but I didn't expect to be in here fucking her, so my ass was unprepared.

"Do you have a cond-..." I knew where that was going, so I cut her off by pushing my dick inside of her. If I said no, there was no way this was happening and her ass would probably move off Earth if I let her get away today. This shit was wrong on so many levels, especially since she didn't know I had a girl, but I wanted her in the worst way. I had to have her.

Pushing her legs back to her face, I held them with one hand as I played with her pussy with my other. The entire time, I was going balls deep in her shit going for broke. Her pussy contracted every time I stroked her shit and it was slowly pulling my nut up. I have no idea when the last time she had sex, but shorty shit was tight and juicy. It felt like an electric shock was going through me each time my dick went inside.

"Fuuuuuckkkk what the fuck you trying to do to me Jonay?" This shit wasn't right and even though I was on top, I felt like the bitch.

"Fuck me from the back." Knowing I could never deny shit she ask for, I pulled out and let her turn over. I'm not sure how long she would have in this position, but I was about to give her the best that I had until I came. That shit wasn't about to be long though. Her pussy juices was dripping off my dick as I stared at her ass in the air. Grabbing her cheeks, I guided my dick inside and dug in. Using her booty as leverage, I slammed into her hard and fast. My eyes started rolling and I knew it was over for my ass.

JONAY...

"I'm sorry." I had no idea why he was apologizing, because this white boy was tearing my pussy up. I didn't even have time to feel weird about it either because the minute he started sucking my nipples, I was ready. It's been so long since I fucked, my pussy was on fire from the touch of his lips against my skin.

"Mmmm this shit is so good. Oh my God." As soon as I got that out, his ass started shaking and snatched out of my pussy fast as hell. I knew then he wasn't wearing a condom. His cum shot out on my ass and I just laid on my stomach. I could feel him getting up to go get a towel and when I heard the water running, the shame kicked in. I didn't know this man from a can of paint. What if he had something? What if he was playing me and only wanted sex? Could he fire me? Panic had kicked in, but I couldn't move because I had nut all over my backside.

61

The warm rag ran across me and I laid there waiting for him to stop, so I could ask a million questions. I must have had cum running down me, because he lifted my ass in the air and wiped me. Before I could say or do anything else, he had his mouth wrapped around my pussy again. I wanted to yell no, we can't do this again, but the shit was feeling so good and I didn't get to cum when we fucked. I noticed he was lying on the bed under me, and I took advantage of that position and rode his face.

His ass locked me down on him and took every bit of the pussy I threw at his ass. I was about to cum again when his ass picked me up off his face and placed me on his dick. It didn't make sense to complain about a condom now, because we already fucked. Leaning forward, I started bouncing up and down on his dick making sure I got my nut this time. Leiland grabbed me by my hair and pulled me to his mouth and kissed me hard as fuck as I rode the shit out that dick.

When my body started shaking again, he grabbed me by waist and locked me down on top of him. His strokes was short since he had me stuck in my position, but they was hard and fast. I could tell he was about to cum because his dick was brick hard inside of me and for a minute, I thought he wasn't going to release me. When he did, I don't know what came over me, but I didn't get up. I kept riding him until I felt him coating my walls with his nut. Since I had already fucked up, I needed to make sure his ass wasn't going nowhere, so I slid off him and did something I never thought I would do. I put that mufuckas dick in my mouth and sucked both of our cum clean off. I never thought I would ever give a white guy head, but his dick was pretty making me want to keep sucking.

It had been a while since I gave head, so I kept going until I got my mojo back. By the time I was done, his legs was crossed and he was pushing me off of him. Laughing, I laid on the side of him and just stared. This man was pretty as fuck and I almost passed him up because he was white. Everything about his ass was perfect and I prayed he wasn't on any bullshit now that he got the pussy.

"Now what?" I looked at him waiting for him to answer, but nothing came out. He stayed silent so long, I thought he was sleep. Finally, he turned and looked at me and my pussy jumped again. I could fuck this man all day and night, but I needed to see where we stood.

"What you mean. We gone order some food and fuck, eat some more and fuck. Imma wear that pussy out until you can't walk." Even though my body shuddered, that's not what I meant.

"That sounds good and all, but I mean now what about us. I don't just walk around having casual sex with people. Hell, I haven't fucked in years. So, I need to know what this is before I continue."

"All you need to know is I got you. We good." I wanted to slap his ass and ask him what he mean we good, that wasn't a damn answer. His ass was sleep and I knew it didn't make sense to say anything now. Turning on my side, I laid there

thinking how much of a dummy I was for this shit here. I've

done some dumb shit in my life, but this one by far took the

cake. Twenty minutes and a million dummies later, I closed

my eyes to go to sleep as well. "I know you're sleep, but that's

probably for the best. If I said this shit to yo face, you

wouldn't believe me no way. From the first day I laid eyes on

you, I knew I loved you. You're going to be mine no matter

how hard yo ass fight it." Since he thought I was sleep, I didn't

respond, but on the inside I was screaming and panicking at

the same time. Love? How the fuck can he love me and he just

met me. This mufucka was giving off psycho signs and I

wanted to run the fuck up out of there. His dick was good as

fuck though, but he just threw me with that shit.

LEILAND...

Looking around the floor, I grabbed my pants and got my phone. I already knew I was going to have a million missed calls from Stacie, but I ain't give a fuck. Clearing my notifications, I looked over at Jonay and smiled as she laid there sleeping. I couldn't even front, shorty was beautiful as fuck and this shit just felt right. Leaning over, I kissed her softly on her mouth. She stirred and looked up at me.

"What time is it?" I didn't want to tell her because I knew she was going to freak out.

"Do it matter? Let's go out and get some food." I tried to slide past that shit, but she wasn't going.

"Leiland, I need to get home so I can get ready for work tomorrow. How long have we been laid up in this room?" Knowing I couldn't hide it from her any longer, I came clean.

"It's kind of already tomorrow. We stayed the night together. Before you go the fuck off, I am the boss and you missing today doesn't bother me. Besides, yo job is right

downstairs." I could see the panic spreading across her face

and I laughed because I knew a shit storm was about to come.

"Why the fuck would you let me sleep that long? I need

to go home and shower and get dressed. I have-..." I cut her

off because she was making a million excuses.

"You have nothing at home but yo friend and liquor.

We're downtown Chicago, I can get you clothes and I have a

hotel full of showers. Stop panicking and shit like you got

something or somebody at home. Now go wash that pussy,

shit can't be stale when I slide back in it." She laughed and ran

to the bathroom. Unlocking my phone, I went to my notes to

send a reminder for someone to clean this room. Maybe I

would make this one off limits.

"You think you run shit, but you wasn't talking tough

when you were professing your undying love for me last

night." I could tell she was trying to read me and see if I

meant any of it, so I played her game.

"Maybe yo ass was dreaming. You did have slob all in my arm pit. The only thing on my mind yesterday was pussy." She seemed satisfied with my answer and jumped in the shower. I was happy, because I wasn't trying to be around here looking like a creep. Even though I meant what I said, I wasn't trying to scare her off.

"You got some good ass body wash in here for it to be a hotel. It smell so good." Even though she was referring to the soap, all I heard was this pussy fresh. Shaking it off, I went to the sink outside the bathroom and grabbed a towel to wash my dick off. "You nasty as hell. How you gone be a rich ass nigga taking a hoe bath?" Laughing, I grabbed a dry towel and patted it dry. The look on her face tripped me out. "What the fuck are you doing?"

"When you wipe shit off, it dries it out. My dick too pretty to be out here chaffed and shit. Throw your clothes on, but not yo panties, that will defeat the purpose." Even though Jonay looked offended, she did what I asked.

"Where are we going?"

"I'm taking you shopping Pretty Woman." As soon as it slipped off my lips, I realized that may not have been the best reference.

"Did you just call me a fucking prostitute?"

"I did, but that's not what I meant. Don't start that fuck you and you think you better than me shit. Take it out on my pockets if you wanna be pissed. Nothing you can do will get me to argue with yo ass today."

"If you don't want to argue, then you don't call the girl you fucked all night and taking shopping a prostitute." She threw her clothes on with an entire attitude and I just stood there and watched her. When she finished, she stood there scathing at me.

"You done? Can we go now?"

"Don't get cute."

"I'm just saying, do you want to sit here and keep moping around like a kid or would you like to go fuck up some commas?" When she finally smiled, we walked out of the room. Stepping off the elevator, I noticed how busy it was in the lobby. It shouldn't have been, because the contractors wasn't supposed to come until tomorrow. I decided to let it go because I didn't want to be sucked into work. Jonay was about to get to know the real me, and I didn't want to jeopardize it.

Throwing my shades on, I held her hand as we walked towards my Tesla. Getting in, I threw my shades on and drove off like this was my bitch and we owned shit out here. She didn't realize it yet, but that's exactly what the fuck it was going to be. My phone started ringing again, and I glanced it. Stacie was blowing me up, but there was no way I was going to answer that shit in front of Jonay.

"Somebody been tearing yo line down since last night. Luckily, I can sleep through anything or that shit would have pissed me off. Get yo hoes in check Mr. Rosstein." Shorty was something else.

"Was that plural? Your ass be tripping man. You need to learn how to just enjoy life. I don't know yo past, but I know mine. We were happy with what we had and we lived. Yo ass out here just existing and shit and you're miserable. Because of it, you make everyone around you miserable. Cut that shit out. Take yo aggression out on my dick if you must, but that's it." She looked at me weird, then out of nowhere she started crying.

"You have no idea how hard my life has been. Yeah, you struggled and shit as well, but black people have a different struggle. My parents went there entire lives living on government assistance and was just fine with that. They never wanted anything more, they never tried to scheme or hustle up extra money. Nothing, they were perfectly fine with us being broke as hell. We couldn't get snacks, clothes, shoes, nothing and kids are fucking cruel.

As soon as I could, I got a job and because I was bringing in a little more money and they didn't want that to go away. So, they fucked me over going to school and I left. I never looked back and I've been pushing through trying to make it ever since. Temp job after temp job and nothing seems to shake. I'm not miserable, I'm broken. I'm tired and I just want something more." I had to look away because the man in me wouldn't allow me to tear up. I couldn't believe shorty had been through so much and no one was there to help her. At least my family had each other. Shit don't seem so bad when you got a family of love. That's the only reason I put up with their bullshit now, because we've always had each other's back.

"Look, I know I can't tell you how to feel and shit, but you have to accept life for what it is. If you feeling your lowest, you can't go anywhere but up. If you're up but feel like you're dropping, then do something to push yo self up. I'm not saying this shit is easy, I'm just saying you can't be around this bitch giving up. I was broke and I made my own opportunities. We've grown closer, but not once have you asked me about a permanent job. Never mentioned it. Shit not gone just fall in yo lap. If you hungry, ask for a fucking meal." When she didn't respond, I knew she heard me. Turning my music up, I slid my hand over to hers and held it. She had no idea, but I was going to help her.

"Don't think I just take life's fuck ups. I did do some college courses. Bills started kicking my ass, so I had to stop going and get a job. I've been doing temp work every since." Jonay tried to say it over the music, but I heard her. Assuming what she said didn't need a response, I left it alone. Wanting to put a smile on her face, I drove to Michigan Avenue and parked outside of Louis Vuitton. "What the fuck are we doing here? You about to do the most ain't you." Smiling, I looked at her and nodded.

"You have no idea how extra a mufucka is. Imma give you one day to forget all the bullshit you been through and show you how you should be treated. Now, you can keep complaining or bring yo ass in this store and get what the fuck you want." Laughing, she jumped out fast as hell and ran over to me. Usually, I open the door for her, but today her ass didn't even wait.

"You know you can't just leave your car out here right?" Grabbing her hand, I walked her towards the store.

"When you got money like me, you can park wherever the fuck you want." Going in the store, my normal guy ran over to me knowing I always spend bread. I could see the shocked look on his face when I saw I wasn't with Stacie.

"Heyyy my favorite money bag. I've been looking for you. This shoe came in and I put one up just for you. It screams Ross." Laughing, I shook my head no.

"Not today Julian, it's all about this shorty right here. I don't give a fuck if she wants the entire store, give her what she wants." Her eyes lit up and she didn't know what to go look at first. Knowing I was going to be in there a while, I sat my ass down and started scrolling through my messages. Seeing my moms had called a few times, I returned her call.

"Son, are you okay?" Shaking my head at her dramatics, I answered.

"Why wouldn't I be?"

"Stacie has been calling me all morning saying you didn't come home last night and you weren't at the hotel today."

"I was there and last I checked I was grown as fuck. You can tell Stacie that you don't run me, I'll see her when I get back."

"What the hell has gotten into you lately? You're acting like that little street kid you tried to be years ago. Bring your butt home this instance and talk to your fiancé." I had to laugh at that shit.

"Ma, that lil street kid I tried to be, is the reason you can play boujie right now. Let's not forget, we was trailer park trash. Stacie is not my fiancé, and I'll talk to her when I get back like I said."

"You're being very disrespectful. I'm about to go to the spa to clear my mind, we will talk when I get back."

"Yeah, go spend my hood money." Hanging up, I laid my head back and closed my eyes. When my phone started ringing again, I knew it was Stacie. Answering, I looked around and made sure Jonay wasn't around me.

"What's up man?"

"Why would you talk to mama like that? If you were going on a trip, why didn't you just tell me that? You had me worried, I couldn't sleep without you there."

"Who said I went out of town? I'm going to tell you like I told her, I'm grown and I don't have to discuss my whereabouts. I'll be back soon and we will talk then."

"How does these look on me?" Jonay ass walked up out of nowhere and I prayed Stacie didn't hear her. I was going to tell her what was going on when I got back. For now, I just wanted everything to stay perfect. My heart was telling me Jonay was who I should be with, but I had years with Stacie. I was never really happy with her, but she was loyal and everyone told me she was who I should be with.

"Are you with a woman? Leiland, who is that in the background?" Not saying a word, I just hung the phone up. Turning it on silent, I looked up at shorty and smiled.

"You already know my dick hard. I know it's a lot of shit, but can you hurry up this is not the only store we going in." When she heard that, she took off running and I looked down at my ringing phone. Not wanting to deal with it, I sent her to voicemail.

JONAY...

"If I didn't know any better, I would think you trying to hide us from the world. You got my ass trapped up in this room like we live together." Even though I was in heaven, me and Leiland had been living out of room 1231 for a week now and he seemed in no rush to leave.

"How the fuck am I hiding you when we been out every day?" He was right, this week had been the best one of my life. We have taken cruises, expensive dinners, parties, and we even went skiing. It was crazy how much you didn't see when you're broke. I never knew a life like this existed, but I still felt as if something was off. Out of all the places he took me, his house wasn't one.

"I want to see where you live and meet your friends and shit. We can't stay in this room forever."

"It's more convenient. We can work and stay together if we at the hotel. I'm not hiding you I just love our getaway.

For once, can you stop complaining." His ass thought I was stupid, but if I didn't know shit else, I knew when someone was lying to me. I don't know why he was sending me off, but he was.

"If I complain so much, why do you want to be around me all day and night? Stop bullshitting me and take me home. If you don't want your friends and family to know that you dating a black girl, just say that. The lil fantasy over right? You're no longer obsessed with the black pussy you've never had." I could see his jaw line jumping, but I wasn't backing down. Not this time. He was going to give me answers or he could leave me the fuck alone.

"Let's go. If you're that fucked up that you can't even let a mufucka spoil you, then I'll take yo ass the fuck home. I have done everything to get you to see what a mufucka was feeling, but you determined to think what you want." If he thought his lil rant was going to make me change my mind, he was wrong. Grabbing my coat, I snatched my purse and walked out the door. He silently followed behind me. As soon as we were on the elevators, I pushed the ground button, but he hit the emergency stop. I turned towards him ready to go the fuck off, when he slammed me against the wall. Before I could curse his ass out, his tongue was pushing its way in my mouth.

I wanted to tell him to get off of me, but his hand was sliding up my body and he had my shit on fire. Releasing my titty from my bra, he bit my nipple and I went crazy. His ass was snatching shit off me aggressively and I did the same for his clothes. I bit his neck so hard I could taste blood in my mouth. Instead of screaming out, he threw his head back like he was enjoying that shit.

Dropping down to my knees, I looked up at him as I took his dick into my mouth. His legs shook and he held on to the railing. I made love to him with my mouth and more than my mouth got wet. I played in my pussy as I took every inch of him inside of my throat. I guess he couldn't take it anymore, so he snatched me up. Placing me around his neck, he tore into my pussy like it was his last meal. Every time I tried to take control, he slammed me against the wall.

Not being able to take anymore, I allowed myself to cum all in his mouth. Without waiting any longer, he dropped me down to his dick and slid inside of me. My pussy grabbed his dick like it belonged to him. In that moment, I knew he was where I belonged and I wasn't going to fight this anymore. My shit contracted and he groaned hard as hell. His dick was slamming inside of me hard as hell and I didn't know how much more I could take.

"Fuck, I'm cumming." Knowing I didn't have long, I gyrated against him causing enough friction to bring my nut up as well. My body started shaking again and we came together. Our breaths was labored and we just stared at each other. I could see how much he cared from the way that he looked at me. He finally released me and I laughed as I started grabbing my clothes. We got dressed and he turned back to me. "I know you might don't believe me, but I love you Jonay."

"I think I love you too. Now take off the emergency break before our dumb ass end up stuck on the elevator." Laughing, he released the break, but the elevator started going down. Someone must have pushed the button and now I had to try and hide my shame until we got back to the room. I prayed they couldn't smell the way he fucked me on that bitch. When the door opened, it was a guy about to get on and a white lady on crutches standing in the lobby. The way Leiland's body froze, I knew our fantasy was over.

"Don't tell me he's not here because his car is outside. You search every inch of this hotel and find him." White lady was going off and I just stared at Leiland. He couldn't even look at me.

"Ma'am, he's right there." When she started hopping over, he finally turned to me.

"I'm sorry shorty, but I'm going to fix this." Before I could ask him what he meant, she was in our face going off on him.

"I thought you were out of town. What the hell is going on and why don't the workers know you are here?" She finally looked at me and gave me the nastiest look she could muster up. "Umm, can you go find you some work to do. That is why you're here right? To get paid. Why are you just standing here, go find something to do while me and my man talk." Any other time, I would have beat her ass, but my heart was stuck in my ass.

"Stacie, that shit ain't caused for and she don't have to leave. Why are you here?" He didn't deny her being his girlfriend and I was done. Walking off, I damn near ran out the door and realized my car wasn't there. "Jonay wait." Not wanting to hear his lies, I took off running towards the train and I didn't stop until I was on it.

All of this shit was a lie. I should have known this shit was too good to be true. What would someone like him want with someone like me. That's why his trifling ass wanted to be in the hotel the entire time. He couldn't take me home because he had a bitch. When my phone started ringing, I looked down and saw it was him. Hitting decline, I went to my settings and placed him on the block list immediately.

It was nothing to talk about. He should have been trying to talk to me the first time he kissed me. Hell, before we fucked. This mufucka came in me multiple times and he had a whole bitch. A disrespectful ass bitch at that. I was too old to be getting played like this. I should have known better, but all those romantic comedies had a bitch thinking shit like that could happen in real life. This was on me, I fucked up and I deserved everything I got. My phone rang again, but I didn't recognize the number, so I answered.

"Hello."

"Yes, this is Stacie and I wanted to make sure you were clear on something just in case it went over your head. You're fired. If you step foot back on our premises, we will have you arrested. Oh, and I will make sure to tell the temp agency to make sure they don't send a homewrecking ghetto bitch the next time someone requests good help."

"Bitch-..." Before I could read her ass, she hung up in my face. The tears fell from my eyes and I tried my best to wipe them away. I refused to break down in front of all these people. Besides, I had been through worst and I always seemed to come out on top. This was just another lying ass mufucka that hurt me, but never again. He could eat a dick on Sunday. Getting off the train, I looked around to make sure no one was following me. To be honest, it made me feel worse knowing he didn't even try to come after me to explain. I walked fast as hell to my apartment building and ran upstairs. As soon as I walked inside, I dropped to the floor and cried my eyes out. I thought he was different, but his bitch ass was

just another lying ass bitch with lighter skin.

LEILAND...

"Why the fuck would you call her? I didn't fire her and I'm not. If she shows up tomorrow, she will get to work. This is not yo hotel, it's my shit and I make the decisions." Stacie had crossed the line and I needed Jonay to come in, so I could talk to her.

"So, you cheated on me with that black bitch and you're mad at me for firing her? How am I wrong? I've been nothing but good to you and I didn't deserve this."

"NEITHER DID SHE! All of this is on me, I get that. Let me ask you this though. Why couldn't she just be a bitch, why do it matter that she's black?" Her expression told me everything I needed to know.

"Why does any of that matter. You cheated on me with her and you're standing here defending her like I mean nothing to you." Pinching the bridge of my nose, I tried to calm down before I said something bad to her ass.

"It matters because you're a fucking racist. What makes you think I could ever love and marry a fucking racist? When my moms couldn't feed all of us because her assistance ran out, it was my black friend who fed me. When my feet was busting out of my shoes and all the kids was laughing at me, it was my black friend that gave me a pair of his Jordans to fit in. You don't get to frown yo nose down on a mufucka because you feel you're better. Hell, truth be told, you wouldn't be with me if I wasn't rich."

"How could you say something like that? I love you Leiland and you know that."

"Naw man, you love my bread and that's why you try to change me every chance you get. We have never truly been happy, but I loved you because you were ambitious and driven. It wasn't until it was too late that I learned you were only that way with my shit. I know we got history and I know I hurt you, and for that, I'm sorry. Just be honest with yourself for once and admit it's my money that keeps you here and it was your sex that kept me. We don't have shit in common."

She started crying, and I felt bad as shit. The only reason I

hadn't walked away before now was because I didn't want to

trade her in for a bigger evil. At least I knew her fucked up

ways and motives, I wouldn't know with someone new. That

was until I met Jonay. I felt more for her in my soul with one

look, then I did with Stacie our entire relationship.

"I'm not letting you do this to us. I'm going home and I

will be waiting for you to get there. You don't see it now, but

we belong together. That girl don't know you like I do and she

doesn't love you like me. She found out about me and took off

running leaving you begging her to return. I found out about

her and I'm standing here fighting for us."

"That alone speaks volumes about you. Why would you

be okay with me hurting you?" Not even waiting for an

answer, I jumped in my car and drove towards Jonay's house. I

needed to talk to her, so I could try to explain.

When I got there, I took a deep breath and got out. I wasn't sure if she would open the door, but I had to try. Heading inside the building, I stopped when I saw a man with a bunch of keys. I wasn't sure if he was the landlord or maintenance, but I was hoping he could help me out.

"Hey, I'll give you a thousand dollars if you let me in my girl's crib. She's mad at me and I just need to talk to her." He looked up at me as if he was trying to see if I was crazy. "I promise I ain't on no bullshit, I just need to talk to her."

"If I even think something is wrong, I will call the police and imma tell them you broke in. What floor?" Smiling, I reached in my pocket and grabbed him two thousand instead.

"Second. I really appreciate this man." When he saw how much I gave him, his ass ain't care about shit no more.

"Aight, just keep it down. Come on." Running up the stairs behind him, I tried my best to figure out what I was going to say. How do you tell someone my bad I didn't tell you about my girlfriend, but I want you? As soon as he unlocked the door, he ran off and I went inside. It was dark and she was lying on the couch. I could hear her sniffling, so I knew she was crying. When she heard the door close, she jumped up and I could see the fire in her eyes. Running over to me, she slapped me so hard I couldn't speak. Even if I wanted to be pissed, her standing in front of me with just a little ass tank top on with no bra on distracted me.

"Get the fuck out of my house." Before I could say anything, she slapped me again. "You think you can come sweet talk me and shit will be good again? You think you can hurt me and I forgive you like it ain't shit. I don't give a fuck how much money you got you don't get to do people like that. NOW GET OUT!" This time, I caught her hand when she went to slap me. Snatching her to me, I crashed my mouth down on hers and kissed her hard. She tried to push me off, but I refused to let go.

When I felt the fight leave her body, I picked her up around my waist and pulled my dick out fast. If I waited too long, she would come to her senses and I didn't need that. I needed her to feel my love with each stroke of my dick. Pushing inside her, I groaned and just sat there. Her pussy sent shocks through me and I needed a minute. Leaning her against the wall, I shoved my dick in her while I held her against the wall. Her tears only made me fuck her harder. Taking my tongue, I used it to lick her tears away.

"Don't cry baby I'm sorry. I'm sorry. Please know that I'm sorry." Each time I said it, I slammed inside of her hard. Her moans and screams made me feel we were okay. She knew where I wanted to be. I didn't need or want Stacie, all I wanted was Jonay. Walking her over to the couch, I pulled her off me and turned her around fast as hell.

Sliding my dick inside of her again, I went for broke in that bitch. I took off and fucked her like it was my last time. Grabbing her titties, I used them as leverage to hold on as I continued to beat that shit up. My dick was swelling up and I knew I didn't have long. I could tell she felt it too because she started throwing that shit back on me hard and fast. She already knew my body and that turned me on more. I held it until I felt her shaking and I let my nut flow all through her pussy. I kept shoving my shit inside until my dick went so soft it fell out. I didn't want to move, but I knew I couldn't keep my weight on top of her. Rolling over, I sat on the couch and laid my head back. I know it was a lot we had to talk about, but I needed her to feel me first. I was hoping that shit softened the blow and it would let her hear me. When I felt the hit to my face, I knew that shit wasn't happening.

"I'm not going to tell you again to get the fuck out of my house." She had her phone in her hand and I knew what that meant. I couldn't believe she would fuck me and still kick me the fuck out.

"You gone call the police on me Jonay?"

"Sure in the fuck am. You have ten seconds or I will hit send and tell them you took my pussy." I couldn't believe she was saying this shit. Was she that fucked up that she would tell them I raped her? When I saw her dialing, I got up and fixed my clothes. Looking at her one last time, I tried to beg her with my eyes. "If you ever come around my building again, know that I will call the cops. Don't try me, I would hate to ruin you." Nodding my head, I walked out of her house defeated.

I never expected this shit to go like this. My plan was to tell Stacie as soon as I left from with Jonay, the only problem was, I could never pull myself away from her. I wanted to be with her all the fucking time and now the shit backfired in my face. Stacie leg was broken, so I never expected them to run into each other. I assumed I had time to fix the shit, but that shit ain't happen.

Turning my radio up, I drove home feeling like shit. When I saw that Stacie actually brought her ass back to my house, I shook my head and just went inside. I didn't have the energy to fight, I just wanted to take my ass to sleep. When I walked inside, her face lit up.

"I knew you would come home. We can fix this if you are willing to try. Let's go to the room and I can show you how much I missed you." I never even looked at her, I just kept walking to the guest room. Slamming the door, I locked it and climbed in the bed. I thought about Jonay until I fell asleep.

JONAY...

2 months later...

Ain't no sunshine when she's gone. It's not warm when she's away. Ain't no sunshine when she's gone and she's always gone too long, anytime she goes away.

"Bitch I know you not in here listening to this sad ass music like you still suicidal. Didn't nobody tell you to go fuck my man and I damn sure didn't tell you to fall for his ass. Now you sitting in here with the white man blues. Bitch do better." I know Nautica was only trying to make me laugh, but nothing came out of my eyes but tears. Wasn't shit funny about none of this shit.

"Not today Nauti, I just want to sleep."

"Fuck that, you wasn't sleep when you was riding that horse to the old town road. Couldn't even tell yo friend you was out there slaying pussy, but now you want some time.

Fuck that. I could have told you not to fall for his ass. Men like that don't fall for women like us."

"No bitch, they don't fall for women like me. Strippers stay coming up on the rich niggas. I wasn't trying to come up though, I thought he really loved me."

"Looovvveeeee. Bitch in two days. If yall don't get that Cinderella bullshit up out of here. I don't care how white he is, yo ass is black and should have known better. That type of shit only happen on tv. Now let's get drunk and talk shit about his ass. Fuck all this sad ass music. Turn this shit the fuck off." Walking over to my phone, she scrolled through my playlist and played Lil Kim. "Now this hoe knew what you was supposed to do with these niggas." I laughed as she went in the kitchen to pour us a drink. When she came back with the cup, she tried to hand it to me but I shook my head no.

"I'm good." When she looked at me, she sat down with her mouth open.

"Friend no. You didn't use a condom?" Shaking my head, I wiped the tears as they fell from my face. Before she could say anything, she went to sit her cup on the table, but saw the envelope. Grabbing it, she picked it up and read the contents. I should have known what she was going to say.

"Bitch, why you ain't tell me we was going to a party. Get yo sad ass up and let's go holla at yo baby daddy."

"I'm not going. Plus, I don't want shit from his ass. I'm not telling him about the baby, he can be happy with his bitch."

"Now friend, who taught you stupid cus I ain't learn that in school? That nigga is rich and you been out here struggling. His bitch fired you and then black balled yo ass, so you can't get a job. How the fuck you gone pay yo bills? This baby is your lottery ticket." It amazed me how easily her gold digging ways came out.

"He paid my rent off. My landlord said I will never have to pay him anything. I don't know what kind of arrangement they made, but he made sure I was straight. Paid off my car note as well."

"While all of that is nice, how the fuck you gone eat? How you gone buy what you need for the baby? You're allowing your emotions to take over. All bullshit aside, that man deserves to know he got a kid. You don't have to take him to child support, but you need to let him be a father. Now is not the time to be emotional." Breaking all the way down, I cried hard as hell. I knew she was right, but I didn't want to see him.

"I don't have shit to wear."

"I thought he took you on a shopping spree."

"He did, but I left all the stuff there."

"Yup, you a big ol dummy. Get up, I'm taking you to get yo shit. Where is it?"

"At the hotel if he hasn't cleaned it out. The hotel opens tomorrow after the grand opening tonight. I'm sure he's cleaned that room up by now. Or his bitch did."

"Well, we going down there. If his ass threw it away, he about to give you some bread to go buy some more." Against my better judgment, I got up and threw on some clothes. Walking downstairs, we got in her car and my ass was damn near shaking. By the time we pulled up, I was having a full blown panic attack.

"I can't go in." Nautica exhaled and opened her door.

"I'll go in, but your ass going to that party."

"If you see him, please don't tell him about the baby, I want to tell him myself." Nodding, she got out and went inside. I kept looking at the door hoping he didn't walk out here trying to talk. Thirty minutes later, Nautica walked out with two bellhops and all my bags. When she got in the car, she went the fuck off.

"Yo hoe ass talking about you didn't want to go in knowing you had all this shit. Fuck you think I got, eight arms." When they were done putting the bags inside, she drove off and then I questioned her.

"Did you see him? What did he say?"

"Damn bitch, I thought you didn't care. He asked me were you out here and I told him no. He walked me upstairs to the room and we fucked." My eyes fell out of my head and she laughed hard as hell. "I'm just playing, but that room looks like he been sleeping there. Nothing about it looks ready for an opening. He gave me all your stuff and told me to tell you he loves you."

"Okay." Now she was looking at me like I was crazy.

"Okay. What the fuck you mean okay. You need to talk to that man. I'm not smart as hell, but shit can't be how you think it is. Just talk to him and let him explain."

"I'll talk to him about the baby and that's it." She left it alone and I was grateful for that. As soon as we got back to my house, we carried all the stuff inside.

"I'm going home to get ready. If you even think about not answering this door, I will break it in. See you in a lil bit." I didn't want to face him, but I knew I didn't have a choice. I didn't want to be the bitter baby mama that kept his child from him, but I didn't want to hear his excuses either. He hurt me and I was done. It was nothing left for us to say. At least that's what I kept telling myself.

LEILAND...

"No, you don't have to worry about that room. I don't want that one open to the public."

"Just for opening? Or is it a time frame on when it will be ready?"

"Room 1231 will never be open to the public, but you will keep it cleaned and maintained. If Jonay Samuels ever tries to check in here, she will be given this room free of charge. Make sure you put her name in the system for this room."

"Okay sir, got it. Anything else?"

"If you see her at the party, make sure you come and find me. Tell everyone else the same thing."

"Okay." Hanging up the phone, I went in my bedroom to get my clothes out. I've been staying at home, but I avoided Stacie like the fucking plague. She refused to leave hoping I would give in, but I haven't. I always assumed Jonay would reach out to me or at least come by the hotel, but she didn't. Shorty didn't even come pick up her check, so I had it sent to her house. Knowing she wouldn't talk to me, I found out her info and paid off everything I could. At least she wouldn't have to worry about most of it, until she found her another job. If I thought she would let me give her some bread, I would do that to. Out of nowhere, it hit me, so I called the HR lady I hired.

"I need you to do me a favor. Can you find out if Jonay had filled out for direct deposit? If so, I need her banking information. Her check was short and I can't find her new address to send it."

"Sure thing Mr. Rosstein, I'll let you know." Hanging up, I smiled. I really hoped it worked. When I cut her check, I never looked at her paperwork. Jumping in the shower, I tried to erase her from my thoughts. I hadn't been back to our room, because it was just too many memories for me. Today was the first time I had been in there since she left. Just as I was starting to go long periods of time without thinking about her, her friend showed up at the hotel. I was washing my balls, when I felt her mouth.

"Stacie, what the fuck are you doing?" She looked up at me and tried to give me a sexy smile.

"You're tense and you're about to have a grand opening. You need to relax and what better way to do that. I know you don't want me and this won't change anything, but let me help you." When her mouth went around my dick again, I said fuck it and closed my eyes. I pictured Jonay's thick lips around my dick and my shit bricked up. It took me no time to explode in Stacie's mouth, but she kept sucking. My shit got right back hard, because I kept her face in my head.

Bending her over in the shower, I slid inside of her with ease. There was no shocks or gripping of my dick, but I pushed Jonay's face back in my mind and took off.

"Fuck baby, I knew you missed this pussy. That's right, fuck me hard baby. Fuck me." Squeezing my eyes shut, I tried to drown out her voice and focus. Pumping harder and harder, I slammed my dick inside of her until I felt my shit swelling up. Pulling out, I turned Stacie around and came on her face. I kept stroking until every last drop had landed. Licking it off, she stared at me as she took me in her mouth again. Normally, I would have no more rounds for her ass, but every time I thought about Jonay, my dick bricked up. She was sucking hard as fuck when my phone rung. Hoping it was HR, I pushed her away and jumped out of the shower.

"Hello."

"I found her bank info; I'm going to email you the forms right now."

"Aight, thanks." Grabbing a towel, I wiped Stacie off my dick and threw a dry towel around me.

"Just like that, you're going to walk out and leave me hanging? I didn't get to cum yet."

"My bad, I got some business to handle real quick." Heading to my guest bedroom, I called the manager at my bank.

"Hey Richard, I need you to transfer a million dollars into this account for me."

"Are you sure? Is it a business and can we do it face to face, so I can make sure your money is protected?"

"You better make sure my shit protected no matter what. It's a personal account and I don't have time to come in today. I'm going to email you an account number and the bank. When it's done, let me know."

"Okay Mr. Rosstein. I'm going to get right on it as soon as you send it over." Going to my email, I forwarded him the same email HR had given me. As soon as I hit send, Stacie was walking in the room. Walking over to me, she pushed me on the bed and climbed on top of me.

"I need to cum. You're not about to leave me hot and bothered like this." Since I had started it, I decided to gone and finish the shit off. Stacie started slow riding me, but I

wasn't for all the love making shit she was trying to do.

Grabbing her by the waist, I picked up the pace and started

slamming my dick inside of her. This time, I didn't think

about Jonay, I just wanted to get it over with. I felt her pussy

contracting, so I knew she was about to cum. As soon she did,

I started pumping hard as hell to build mine up. It seemed

like just as mine was about to come up, my phone rang again.

Laughing, I pushed her off me. That must have been a sign

and I was going to take that shit. Grabbing my phone, I

answered it and walked out of the room.

"It's done sir."

"Alright thank you Richard, I got a nice bonus for you."

Hanging up, I looked at Stacie coming towards me again.

"Just let it go. I had to force myself to cum and the

phone rang again. The shit not meant to be. Go get dressed

before we're late for the party."

"So, fuck me. You not going to make sure I'm satisfied?"

"It's not my job to make sure you good. Now, you can go get dressed and come on, or I can go without you." Smacking her lips, she went in the room to get dressed and I did the same. Throwing on a T shirt with some jeans, I topped it off with a long blazer that came to my knees. I slid on my custom Loub's and I was ready to go. When I walked out of my room, Stacie was there waiting on me. I had to laugh, because I was definitely going to leave her if she wasn't ready. Walking downstairs, we jumped in my Phantom and I took off towards the hotel. I was nervous as fuck, but not about my opening.

I had no idea if Jonay was going to come or not. I sent her an invite, but she didn't respond or RSVP. I put her ass on the list anyway and prayed she walked her ass through the door. When we got inside, everyone was congratulating me and everything looked as good as I hoped. Jonay had did a great job on the shit she ordered and I was pleased with the outcome. Walking away from Stacie, I headed over to my brother.

"This mufucka is nice bro. Your girl did well, when you gone propose to her ass?"

"We not together anymore."

"Since when? Five minutes ago, you just walked in with her ass."

"Yeah I know. She's refusing to be dumped. I fell for one of my employees, but I forgot to tell her I had a chick." We both laughed at me saying I forgot.

"You know damn well your ass ain't tell her on purpose. You talking about the black girl everybody been whispering about? Ma refuses to even say the girl's name."

"Yeah. Shorty got my ass and now, I can't even talk to her to try and explain the shit."

"Damn you sound whipped as fuck. If it's all like that, go to her then bro. Make her ass listen and work that shit out."

"It ain't that simple. She told me if I come near her again, she's going to call the police. I don't need that kind of publicity right now. I've made sure she was straight, but she won't hear me out."

"Damn, that's fucked up. This shit worst than Jack dying on Rose at the end of Titanic. I kept hoping his ass floated or drifted up on land somewhere, but nope. His ass was dead dead."

"Get the fuck out of here Len, yo ass is nuts. I ain't gone lie, it do feel like that though. You ever found something that you knew would change yo life and then it was gone?"

"Hell naw, so you better pray I don't see her ass or imma jump on that shit. You around here talking like she got unicorns in her pussy. I ain't never had none of that before." We were laughing hard as hell when my face went serious.

"Damn what happened, your entire expression just changed." I didn't respond, I just walked towards her. She had on a red fitted dress and it was hugging the shit out of her body. The closer I got, the more I could feel her. It's like she was touching me all over my damn body.

"If you think you're about to go to her, you got me mistaken." Looking over at Stacie, I shook my head.

"You mean I got you fucked up and I guess I do." Before I could push her ass out the way, Nautica walked up and blocked Stacie.

"Imma need you to understand I got these hands. I will drag yo ass all up and threw this party. Back off lil bitch. Back off."

I laughed at Nautica as I made my way to Jonay. She was looking around for me and we finally locked eyes. She dropped her head to the ground and I damn near tripped I was walking to her so fast. Before I could say anything to her, Stacie came out of nowhere.

"Hey Leiland, you wanna go upstairs and finish what we started earlier?" Jonay took off running and I wanted to slap her lips off her face. Instead, I ran after Jonay. She was the only mufucka I knew that could run a marathon in heels. I had to actually run to keep up.

"Where the fuck you going Jonay?"

"This was a mistake; I shouldn't have come."

"Or, you can let me take you upstairs so you can cum." I could feel her body shiver and I wanted her bad as fuck.

"I just need to talk to you. Is there somewhere we can talk?" Nodding, I pulled her on the elevator to our room. "I'm not trying to have sex Leiland, I just really need to talk to you."

"Understood." Unlocking the door, I walked inside and sat on the bed. I had no idea what she wanted, but she was nervous as hell.

"If it's money you need, I already deposited a million dollars into your account."

"Why would you do that?"

"So, you will never need anybody for shit. I told you I got you and ain't shit changed."

"I'm pregnant Leiland." The emotions that went through my body was unexplainable. She took it as me being upset and ran towards the door. "I'm sorry, I will take care of the baby on my own. Forget I told you."

"Marry me." She turned around and looked at me like I was crazy.

"What!"

"Marry me Jonay."

"Why? We only known each other for a little bit. You got a girl and now I'm pregnant."

"I loved you from the first time I laid eyes on you. It has nothing to do with you being pregnant. I don't want Stacie and I've told her that. You're who I want and I don't ever want to live without yo ass. So, marry me." She started crying and ran over to me.

"Okay."

"Good, now you can send my bread back."

"Shid, I ain't that dumb." Laughing, I kissed her and started taking her dress off. Fuck that party, I was going to lay inside my girl until my shit went soft and gummy. Nothing else in this moment mattered but her. I've had a lot of things, but I've never had a love like this.

THE END...

KEEP UP WITH LATOYA NICOLE

Like my author page on fb @misslatoyanicole

My fb page Latoya Nicole Williams

IG Latoyanicole35

Twitter Latoyanicole35

Snap Chat iamTOYS

Reading group: Toy's House of Books

Email latoyanicole@yahoo.com

OTHER BOOKS BY LATOYA NICOLE (AVAILABLE ON AMAZON)

NO WAY OUT: MEMOIRS OF A HUSTLA'S GIRL 1-2

GANGSTA'S PARADISE 1-2

ADDICTED TO HIS PAIN (STANDALONE)

LOVE AND WAR: A HOOVER GANG AFFAIR 1-4

CREEPING WITH THE ENEMY: A SAVAGE STOLE MY HEART PART 1-2

I GOTTA BE THE ONE YOU LOVE (STANDALONE)

THE RISE AND FALL OF A CRIME GOD: PHANTOM AND ZARIA'S STORY 1-2

ON THE 12TH DAY OF CHRISTMAS MY SAVAGE GAVE TO ME

A CRAZY KIND OF LOVE: PHANTOM AND ZARIA

14 REASONS TO LOVE YOU: A LATOYA NICOLE ANTHOLOGY

SHADOW OF A GANGSTA

THAT GUTTA LOVE 1-2

LOCKED DOWN BY HOOD LOVE 1-2

THE BEARD GANG CHRONICLES 2 (THE TEASE)

THROUGH THE FIRE: A STANDALONE NOVEL

DAUGHTER OF A HOOD LEGEND 1-2

CRAVING THE LOVE OF A THUG 1-2

SON OF A CRIME GOD, DAUGHTER OF A HOOVER THE

WEDDING